The A to Z

Animal Joke Book

From **Aardvark** to **Zebra**!

Illustrated by Vasco Icuza

Kane Miller
A DIVISION OF EDC PUBLISHING

The A to Z Animal Joke Book

If you're wild about jokes – and love
nothing more than making others laugh,
then this is the perfect book for you!

The A to Z Animal Joke Book is a rib-tickling
collection of over 300 animal-themed one-liners.
The jokes are ordered alphabetically, so you can
chuckle your way from A to Z, or search for a joke
about your favorite animal. From an amusing
aardvark to zany zebras, the laughs don't stop!

The A to Z Animal Joke Book is all you need
to become a joke-telling beast!

A

Q What do you call a thick-skinned **AARDVARK**?

A A hardvark!

Q What do you call an **AFGHAN HOUND** left in the cold?

A A chili dog!

Q Why shouldn't you tease an **ALLIGATOR**?

A Because it might come back to bite you in the end!

Q Why did the **ANACONDA** cross the road?

A To get to the other s-s-s-side!

Q What part of an **ANGELFISH** weighs the most?

A Its scales!

HA HA!

4

Q What do you call an **ANT** wearing its best clothes?

A Eleg-ant!

Q Why don't **ANTEATERS** ever get sick?

Because they're full of ant-ibodies!

Q What is an **ANTELOPE'S** favorite fruit?

A c-antelope!

Q What do **ARCTIC FOXES** eat for lunch?

Brrrrrrrritos!

Q How do you raise a baby **ASIAN ELEPHANT**?

With a forklift!

Q Why do **BABOONS** have large nostrils?

A Because they have big fingers!

HAHAHA!

Q Why did the **BASKING SHARK** cross the ocean?

A To get to the other tide!

Q What do **BATS** do for exercise?

A Aero-bat-ics!

Q Why was the little **BEAR** so spoiled?

A Because its mother panda'd to its every whim!

Q What did the **BEAVER** say to the tree?

A "It's been nice gnawing you!"

Q What happened when two **BEDBUGS** met in an old mattress?

A They got married in the spring!

Q What do you call a **BEETLE** that loves to dance?

A A jitterbug!

Q Why did the **BISON** get into trouble at school?

A Because it misbe-hoofed!

HAH!

Q How do **BLACK BEARS** keep their dens cool in the summer?

A They turn on the bear-conditioning!

Q What did the **BLACK WIDOW SPIDER** eat in Paris?

A French flies!

B

Q Where do **BLUE WHALES** go to get weighed?

A The whale weigh station!

Q Why don't **BORDER COLLIES** sleep well?

A They are up all night counting sheep!

CACKLE!

Q What did the **BORDER TERRIER** do at the flea circus?

A It stole the show!

Q How does a pod of **BOTTLENOSE DOLPHINS** make a decision?

A They flipper coin!

Q What happens when you cross a **BUDGERIGAR** with a shark?

A You get a bird that talks your ear off!

B

 What did the **BUFFALO** say to his son when he left for school?

Bi-son!

 What do you call the stuff between a **BULL SHARK'S** teeth?

Slow swimmers!

 What do you get if you cross a **BULLDOG** with a calculator?

A pet you can count on!

 Why did the **BUMBLEBEE** get married?

Because it had found its honey!

 Why couldn't the **BUTTERFLY** go to the dance?

Because it was a moth ball!

HE HE!

C

Q What do **CAMELS** use to hide themselves?

A Camel-flage!

BWAHAHA!

Q How do **CAPYBARAS** eat spaghetti?

A With their mouths, just like everyone else!

Q What do you call the **CASSOWARY** police?

A The Claw Enforcement Agency!

Q What happened to the **CAT** who swallowed a ball of yarn?

A She had a litter of mittens!

Q What is the definition of a **CATERPILLAR**?

A A worm in a fur coat!

C

Q What do you get if you cross a **CENTIPEDE** and a parrot?

A walkie-talkie!

Q What do you call a wealthy **CHAMELEON**?

A chameleon-aire!

TEE-HEE!

Q Which side of a **CHEETAH** has the most spots?

The outside!

Q How did the **CHICKEN** wake up so early?

It had an alarm cluck!

Q How do **CHIMPANZEES** get downstairs quickly?

They slide down the banana-ster!

C

CHORTLE!

Why is it so hard to be friends with a **CHIPMUNK**?

They drive everyone nuts!

How do you know when a **CLOUDED LEOPARD** has eaten a duck?

It has a down-in-the-mouth look!

What happened to the cat that ate a **CLOWN FISH**?

It felt a little funny for some time afterward!

What's smarter than a talking **COCKROACH**?

A spelling bee!

What is the **COMMON TOAD'S** favorite flower?

A croak-us!

C

What did the **COUGAR** say when it lost all its money?

"Boo-hoo, I'm paw!"

How long do **COWS** fall in love for?

For heifer and heifer!

What do you call a **CRANE FLY** with criminal tendencies?

A baddy long legs!

Who gives **CROCODILES** presents at Christmas?

Santa Jaws!

What's the best way to communicate with a **CUTTLEFISH**?

Drop it a line!

 Why are **DACHSHUNDS** good actors?

They are all Oscar wieners!

What do **DALMATIANS** say after dinner?

"That really hit the spot!"

What do you call a **DEER** with no eyes?

No-eye-deer!

SNICKER!

Why did the **DINGO** cross the road twice?

Because it was a double crosser!

What did the **DOLPHIN** say when it bumped into the octopus?

"I'm sorry, I didn't do it on porpoise!"

Q What do you get when you cross a **DONKEY** with a motorcycle?

A A Yam-Hee-Haw!

Q What game do **DORMICE** love to play?

A Hide-and-squeak!

GUFFAW!

Q What do you call a **DRAGONFLY** without wings?

A A dragonwalk!

Q What time did the **DUCK** wake up in the morning?

A At the quack of dawn!

Q What does a **DUNG BEETLE** put on its food?

A Salt and pooper!

Why can't you keep a sick **EAGLE**?

Because it's ill-eagle!

What do you call it when **EARTHWORMS** take over the world?

Global worming!

What did the **EARWIG** say as the plane took off?

"Ear we go!"

What do you get if you cross an **ECHIDNA** with a giraffe?

A 12-foot-tall toothbrush!

Why did the **ELECTRIC EEL** always look amazed?

Because it found everything shocking!

E

Q Why is an **ELEPHANT** in the kitchen like a house on fire?

A The sooner you put it out, the better!

Q Who did the **ELK** invite to its birthday party?

A Its nearest and deer-est friends!

Q What did one **EMPEROR PENGUIN** say to the other?

A Nothing, it gave it the cold shoulder!

Q Why did the **EMU** cross the road?

A To prove it wasn't a chicken!

HAW-HAW!

Q What do you get if you cross an **ENGLISH SETTER** with a puffin?

A dog that lays pooched eggs!

Q Why was the **FALCON** on its knees with its head bowed?

A Because it's a bird of prey!

Q Which is a **FERRET'S** favorite band?

A The Ferretones!

GIGGLE!

Q What do you get if you cross an elephant with a **FIN WHALE**?

A A submarine with a built-in snorkel!

Q Where do **FIRE-BELLIED TOADS** leave their hats and coats?

A In the croak-room!

Q What do **FIREFLIES** eat at lunchtime?

A A light meal!

F

Q Why are **FISH** so smart?

Because they live in schools!

Q What music do **FISHING CATS** listen to when hunting?

Anything catchy!

Q What's the opposite of a **FLAMINGO**?

A flamin-stop!

Q Why do **FLATFISH** live in salt water?

Pepper makes them sneeze!

BWAHAHA!

Q What is the difference between a **FLEA** and a coyote?

One prowls on the hairy, and the other howls on the prairie!

F

Q What do you call a **FLOUNDER** wearing a tie?

A So-fish-ticated!

GUFFAW!

Q What is the difference between a **FLY** and a bird?

A A bird can fly, but a fly can't bird!

Q Which ballet do **FLYING SQUIRRELS** love?

A *The Nutcracker*!

Q How are a **FOX TERRIER** and a marine biologist alike?

A One wags a tail, and the other tags a whale!

Q What do **FOXES** call rabbits?

A Fast food!

Q What is a **FRENCH BULLDOG'S** favorite musical instrument?

A trombone!

Q How does a **FRENCH POODLE** say hello?

"Bone-jour!"

Q What do you call a **FRILLED LIZARD** that spits rhymes?

A rap-tile!

Q What happened to the illegally parked **FROG**?

It got toad away!

Q Why did the **FUR SEAL** blush?

Because it saw the ocean's bottom!

 Where do **GECKOS** go if they lose their tail?

A re-tail store!

Which fruit do **GEESE** love to eat?

Goose-berries!

What did the **GIANT CLAM** say when it got stuck?

"Kelp! Kelp!"

 Why couldn't the **GIANT PANDA** decide what to eat?

It was bamboo-zled!

Where do you find a **GIANT SNAIL**?

At the end of a giant's finger!

CACKLE!

 Why are **GIBBONS** like bananas?

They both have appeal!

 Why did the **GIRAFFE** do badly in school?

It always had its head in the clouds!

What is the quickest way to make a **GLOWWORM** happy?

 Cut off its tail and it will be de-lighted!

What does a **GNU** read in the morning?

A gnus-paper!

TEE-HEE!

What do you call a **GOAT** who likes to dress as a clown?

A silly billy!

23

G

Q How are **GOLDEN RETRIEVERS** and pennies alike?

A They both have a head and a tail!

Q What is the first thing **GORILLAS** learn at school?

A Their a-pey-cees!

Q Which sport do **GRASSHOPPERS** love?

A Cricket!

CHORTLE!

Q Why did the **GRAY FOX** keep saying "moo"?

Because it was trying to learn a new language!

Q What should you do if a **GREAT DANE** swallows a dictionary?

A Take the words out of its mouth!

Q What did the **GREAT WHITE SHARK** say to the whale?

A "What are you blubbering about?"

Q Why don't **GREYHOUNDS** make good dancers?

A Because they have two left feet!

Q What do you call a **GRIZZLY BEAR** with no ears?

A A grizzly b!

Q Where should you take a sick **GROUNDHOG**?

A To the hog-spital!

Q What should you do if you hear a **GUINEA PIG** squeaking?

A Oil it!

Q How did the **HAMMERHEAD SHARK** do on the test?

A It nailed it!

Q Where do **HAMSTERS** go on vacation?

A Ham-sterdam!

HA HA!

Q What is a **HEDGEHOG'S** favorite snack?

A Prickly pears!

Q What do you call a baby **HERMIT CRAB**?

A A little nipper!

Q How can you get a **HIPPOPOTAMUS** to do whatever you want?

A Use hippo-notism!

Q What do **HONEYBEES** chew?

Bumble gum!

Q What is the difference between a **HORSE** and a duck?

One goes quick, and the other goes quack!

Q How do you catch a **HOWLER MONKEY**?

Climb a tree and act like a banana!

Q What do **HUMBOLDT PENGUINS** wear on their heads?

Ice caps!

Q Why do **HUMMINGBIRDS** hum?

Because they don't know the words!

What did the **IMPALA** say to its kids?

"Hurry up, my deers!"

Why do **INDIAN ELEPHANTS** have wrinkled skin?

Have you ever tried ironing one?

What do you call an **INSECT** with four wheels and a trunk?

A Volkswagen Beetle!

What do you call a young **IRISH SETTER** in the Arctic?

A pup-sicle!

Why did the **IRISH WOLFHOUND** chase its tail?

It was trying to make ends meet!

SNICKER!

Q What did the **JACK RUSSELL** say after it did a backflip?

A "That was paw-some!"

HAW-HAW!

Q How do **JACKALS** greet each other?

A "Howl do you do?"

Q Why was the **JACKRABBIT** upset?

A It was having a bad hare day!

Q What should you do if there is a **JAGUAR** on your bed?

A Sleep on the sofa!

Q Where do **JELLYFISH** sleep when they're camping?

A In tent-acles!

K

Q What kind of music do sophisticated **KANGAROOS** listen to?

Hop-era!

Q What do you call a lonely **KEEL-BILLED TOUCAN**?

A keel-billed one-can!

Q Where does a **KILLER WHALE** go for braces?

A The orca-dontist!

Q When's the wrong time to reason with a **KING COBRA**?

When it is having a hissy fit!

Q Why don't **KING CRABS** do well on exams?

Because they are always below C-level!

CHUCKLE!

Q What song do **KING PENGUINS** sing on birthdays?

A "Freeze a Jolly Good Fellow!"

Q How do you catch a unique **KINGFISHER**?

A Unique up on it!

Q When is the best time to buy a **KIWI**?

A When it's going cheep!

Q Why did the **KOALA** eat so much eucalyptus?

A It simply couldn't leaf it alone!

Q What do you call a **KOMODO DRAGON** with cotton in each ear?

A Anything you want – it can't hear you!

L

Q What did the **LABRADOODLE** say to the flea?

A "Stop bugging me!"

Q Where does a **LAMB** go when it needs a haircut?

A To the baa-baa shop!

Q What do **LEOPARD SEALS** call fish riding skateboards?

A Meals on wheels!

GIGGLE!

Q Why can't **LEOPARDS** escape from the zoo?

A Because they're always spotted!

Q What's the difference between an injured **LION** and a wet day?

A One roars with pain, and the other pours with rain!

Q What do you call a very fast **LLAMA**?

A A llama-ghini!

HA HA!

Q What does a **LOBSTER** say when it answers the phone?

A "Shello!"

Q What does a **LOGGERHEAD SEA TURTLE** have for lunch?

A Peanut butter and jellyfish sandwiches!

Q What is a **LONG-EARED OWL'S** favorite class at school?

A Owl-gebra!

Q What do you call a **LYNX** on the beach at Christmastime?

A Sandy Claws!

M

Q What is a **MACAW'S** favorite game?

A Hide-and-speak!

Q Where do **MACKEREL** sleep?

A On the seabed!

Q What did the little **MAGPIE** say to the big **MAGPIE**?

A "Peck on someone your own size!"

Q What do you call a clever **MALLARD**?

A A wise quacker!

Q Why are **MANATEES** so polite?

A Because they know their manas!

Q How does a **MANDRILL** make hamburgers?

A It puts them on the gorilla!

Q What do you get if you cross a **MARINE TOAD** with a ferry?

A A hopper-craft!

Q What do you call a **MARMOSET** with a wand and robe?

A Hairy Potter!

Q How did the kitten become a member of a **MEERKAT** gang?

A They had no idea it was a mere cat!

Q Where do **MICE** park their boats?

A At the hickory dickory dock!

35

Q Why was the **MILLIPEDE** always late?

A It took it so long to get its shoes on!

Q How did the octopus make the **MINKE WHALE** laugh?

A With ten-tickles!

Q Why did the **MOLE** bite a dog?

A It was feeling mole-icious!

Q How did the **MOLLUSK** get into college?

A On a scallop-ship!

BWAHAHA!

Q What do you do if a **MONGOOSE** swallows your pencil?

A Use a pen!

Q What do you call a **MONITOR LIZARD** that can pick up a car?

A Anything it wants!

Q What do you call an exploding **MONKEY**?

A A baboom!

Q What type of **MOOSE** likes to suck blood?

A A moose-quito!

Q What is the difference between a **MOSQUITO** and a fly?

A You can't zip your mosquito!

Q What's the biggest **MOTH** in the world?

A A mam-moth!

M

Q What is as big as a **MOUNTAIN GORILLA** but weighs nothing?

A Its shadow!

Q How does a **MOUNTAIN LION** paddle its canoe?

A It uses its r-oar!

Q Why was the **MOUSE** afraid of the water?

A Catfish!

Q Why do **MUD CRABS** only think of themselves?

A Because they are very shellfish!

Q What do you call a **MUSSEL** that can fly?

A A shell-icopter!

CACKLE!

38

How do baby **NARWHALS** get their mother's attention?

They nar-wail real loud!

What do **NATTERJACK TOADS** drink?

Croaka-cola!

Why did I name my pet **NEWT** "Tiny"?

Because it is my newt!

What TV show does a **NIGHTHAWK** never miss?

The feather forecast!

What do you give a sick **NIGHTINGALE**?

Tweet-ment!

HAHAHA!

Q How are **NILE CROCODILES** and computers similar?

A They both have lots of bites!

Q Where do **NORTHERN ELEPHANT SEALS** go to see movies?

A To the dive-in!

Q How does a **NORTHERN SEAHORSE** quickly get from one place to another?

A It scallops!

Q Why did the young **NORWEGIAN FOREST CAT** go to medical school?

A It wanted to be a first aid kit!

Q Where did the **NURSE SHARK** go on vacation?

A Fin-land!

HE HE!

Q Why is it so exhausting talking to an **OCELOT**?

A Because they ocelot of questions!

Q Who held the baby **OCTOPUS** for ransom?

A Squid-nappers!

Q What does an **ORANGUTAN** attorney study?

A The law of the jungle!

Q What do you call a baby **ORCA**?

A A little squirt!

SNICKER!

Q Why did the **OSPREY** miss school?

A Because it was feeling under the feather!

O

What happened when the giraffe and **OSTRICH** ran a race?

It was neck and neck!

What type of cars do **OTTERS** drive?

Otter-mobiles.

HAW-HAW!

What do you call an **OWL** with a sore throat?

A bird that doesn't give a hoot!

What happened to the **OX** that got lost?

Nobody's herd!

What do you get when you cross an owl and an **OYSTER**?

Pearls of wisdom!

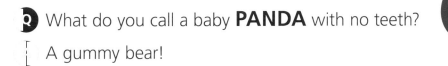

P

Q What do you call a baby **PANDA** with no teeth?

A A gummy bear!

LOL!

Q Why don't **PANTHERS** play cards in the jungle?

A Because there are too many cheetahs!

Q What is orange and sounds like a **PARROT**?

A A carrot!

Q Did you hear the story about the **PEACOCK**?

A It's a beautiful tail!

Q What kind of fish does a **PELICAN** eat?

A Whatever fits the bill!

Q What do you call a happy **PENGUIN**?

A A pen-grin!

CHORTLE!

Q What do you call a **PIG** who was arrested for bad driving?

A A road hog!

Q Where does a rich **PONY** live?

A In the best neigh-borhood!

Q How do you wash a **POODLE**?

A With sham-poodle!

Q What did the **PORCUPINE** say to the cactus?

A "Are you my mommy?"

Q

Q Why are **QUAILS** so vain?

A Because they are quail-ity birds!

Q Who is the **QUEEN BEE** married to?

A Her hub-bee!

Q How did the **QUEEN SNAKE** sign its love letters?

A It sealed them with a hiss!

Q Why did the **QUETZAL** fall from the sky?

A It broke the claw of gravity!

SNICKER!

Q What do you get if you cross a **QUOKKA** with an alien?

A A Mars-upial!

R

Q What did the carrot say to the **RABBIT**?

A "Wanna grab a bite?"

Q What type of car does a **RACCOON** drive?

A A fur-rari!

Q Where do **RAINBOW FISH** go to borrow money?

A The prawn broker!

Q What is a **RAM'S** favorite newspaper?

A *The Wool Street Journal*!

Q What kind of cheese do **RATS** put on pizza?

A Mouse-arella!

HAH!

46

Q How does a **RATTLESNAKE** shoot something?

A With a boa and arrow!

Q What do you get when you cross a **RAVEN** with a mad dog?

A A ravin' lunatic!

Q What do you call a **RED FOX** with a toolbox?

A Mr. Fox-it!

Q What would happen if **RED-KNEED TARANTULAS** were as big as horses?

A If one bit you, you could ride it to the hospital!

GUFFAW!

Q Why don't **RED PANDAS** eat sandwiches?

A They can't bear them!

Q What do **REINDEER** eat for breakfast?

A bowl of deer-ios!

BWAHAHA!

Q What do you get when you cross a **RHINOCEROS** and a goose?

A An animal that honks before it runs you over!

Q Where do **RIVER DOLPHINS** wash their faces?

A In a river basin!

Q Where do **RIVER OTTERS** keep their money?

A In a river-bank!

Q Why did the **ROADRUNNER** cross the playground?

A To get to the other slide!

R

Q What does a 500-pound **ROBIN REDBREAST** say?

A "Here, kitty, kitty, kitty!"

Q Why do **ROCKHOPPER PENGUINS** carry fish in their beaks?

A Because they don't have any pockets!

CACKLE!

Q Why didn't anyone recognize the **ROSEATE COCKATOO**?

A Because it was in da-skies!

Q What is a **ROSE-RINGED PARAKEET'S** favorite kind of cookie?

A Chocolate chirp!

Q What happens when a **ROTTWEILER** swallows a clock?

A It gets ticks!

Q What do you get when you cross a **SAINT BERNARD** with a crocodile?

A An animal that bites you and then goes to fetch help!

Q Why did the **SALAMANDER** feel lonely?

A Because it was newt to the area!

TEE-HEE!

Q Why are **SALMON** so gullible?

A They fall for things hook, line and sinker!

Q What do you call a **SCORPION** in the Arctic?

A Lost!

Q What's a **SEA LION'S** favorite subject in school?

A Ar-ar-ar-art!

S

HA HA!

Q Why do **SEA TURTLES** love their cell phones?

Because they are constantly taking shell-fies!

Q How does a **SEA URCHIN** find things on the Internet?

A It keeps on sea-urchin!

Q Why do **SEAGULLS** like to live by the sea?

A Because if they lived by the bay they would be baygulls!

Q Did you hear about the **SEAHORSE** that said it could fly?

It was just squidding!

Q How do you make a **SEAL** stew?

A Keep it waiting!

S

Q What vitamin do **SHARKS** take to stay healthy?

A Vitamin sea!

Q Where did the **SHEEP** go on vacation?

A The Baaaa-hamas!

Q Why did the **SHIH TZU** have to appear in court?

A Because it got a barking ticket!

Q Why don't **SHRIMP** play tennis?

A Because they are afraid of the net!

HAHAHA!

Q Why did the **SIAMESE CAT** wear a pretty dress?

A Because it was feline fine!

Q How many **SKUNKS** does it take to make a really big stink?

A phew!

Q What do **SLOTHS** like to read?

Snooze-papers!

Q What is the definition of a **SLUG**?

A snail with a housing problem!

Q What did the **SNAIL** say when he got on the turtle's shell?

"Wheeeeeeeeeece!"

Q What do you get if you cross a **SNAKE** with a pie?

A pie-thon!

S

Q What do you call a famous **SNAPPING TURTLE**?

A A shell-ebrity!

Q What is a **SNOWY OWL'S** favorite dessert?

A Mice cream!

Q Did you hear about the book written by a **SPARROW**?

A It flew off the shelves!

Q Why do **SPECTACLED BEARS** have fur coats?

A Because they would look silly in ski jackets!

HAH!

Q What do **SPIDER** knights wear?

A A coat of arms!

54

Q What did the **SQUID** say on its birthday?

A "Today is going to be ink-redible!"

Q How do you catch a **SQUIRREL**?

A Climb a tree and act like a nut!

Q What does a **STAG BEETLE** hang on its Christmas tree?

A Horn-aments!

Q What do you call an unconvincing **STICK INSECT**?

A Unreali-stick!

Q What do you get if you kiss a **SWAN**?

A A peck on the cheek!

HE HE!

Q What type of books do **TAWNY OWLS** love to read?

A Hooo-dunnits!

Q Why do **TERMITES** never have any money?

A Because they eat themselves out of house and home!

GIGGLE!

Q What's the difference between a **TIGER** and a lion?

A A tiger has the mane part missing!

Q What do you call a girl with a **TOAD** on her head?

A Lily!

Q What do **TORTOISES** do on their birthdays?

A They shell-ebrate!

What does a **TOUCAN** say when it wants to pay for something?

Put it on my bill!

Why are **TREE FROGS** always happy?

Because they eat whatever bugs them!

What did the **TRUMPETFISH** say to the sea urchin?

"With friends like these, who needs anemones?"

What do you get if you cross a **TURKEY** with a ghost?

A poultry-geist!

What does a **TURTLE** need to ride a bike safely?

A shell-met!

HA HA!

U

Q What is an **UMBRELLABIRD** after it is five days old?

A Six days old!

Q Why was the **UNDERWING MOTH** so unpopular?

A Because it kept picking holes in everything!

Q Where do **UNICORNFISH** go to practice yoga?

A The river bend!

Q What does an **UPLAND BUZZARD** bring on an airplane?

A A carri-on bag!

Q Why did the **URAL OWL** invite all its friends over?

A It couldn't bear to be owl by itself!

CACKLE!

Q What is a **VAMPIRE BAT'S** favorite type of dog?

A bloodhound!

Q Where do **VERVET MONKEYS** learn about gossip?

They hear it on the ape vine!

Q What is a **VIPER'S** best subject?

A Hiss-tory!

Q How does a **VOLE** feel after taking a shower?

Squeaky clean!

Q What is a **VULTURE'S** favorite kind of underwear?

Thermals! They're always flying in them!

Q How do sick **WALLABIES** get better?

A They have hop-erations!

BWAHAHA!

Q What did the **WALRUS** say when it was confused?

A "I moustache you a question, but I'll shave it for later!"

Q What happens when you put a **WARTHOG** in a musical?

A It squeals the show!

Q What's the difference between a **WEASEL** and a stoat?

A One is weasely identifiable, the other is stoatally different!

Q What is a **WHALE'S** favorite meal?

A Fish and ships!

Q What's the difference between a car and a **WHITE RHINO**?

A A car only has one horn!

Q What is a **WILD BOAR'S** best color?

A Ma-hog-any!

Q What time is it when a **WILDEBEEST** sits in your canoe?

A Time to get a new canoe!

Q Why was the **WOLF** arrested in the butcher's shop?

A It was chop-lifting!

Q What do you get if you cross a **WOODPECKER** with a carrier pigeon?

A A bird that knocks before delivering its message!

LOL!

 CHORTLE!

Q Why does a **XOLOITZCUINTLI** run in circles?

A Because it's hard to run in squares!

Q What did one **X-RAY FISH** say to the other?

A "Sometimes I don't know what I see in you!"

Q What do you call a **YAK** astrologer?

A Zodi-yak!

Q What's the difference between a guitar and a **YELLOWFIN TUNA**?

A You can tuna guitar, but you can't tuna fish!

Q What happened to the **YORKSHIRE TERRIER** who only ate garlic?

A Its bark was much worse than its bite!

Q What's the difference between a **ZEBRA** and a horse?

A zebra has its pajamas on!

HAHAHA!

Q Why did the **ZEBRA FINCH** get into trouble at school?

It was caught tweeting on a test!

Q What did the **ZEBRA LONGWING BUTTERFLY** learn at school?

Moth-matics!

Q What do you call a **ZEBRA SHARK** without stripes?

A shark, of course!

Q What object holds the most **ZOOPLANKTON**?

A whale-barrow!

HA HA!

BWAHAHA!

CACKLE!

HE HE!

LOL!

First American Edition 2020
Kane Miller, A Division of EDC Publishing
Copyright © Green Android Ltd 2019
Illustrated by Vasco Icuza

For information contact:
Kane Miller, A Division of EDC Publishing
P.O. Box 470663
Tulsa, OK 74147-0663
www.kanemiller.com
www.edcpub.com
www.usbornebooksandmore.com

Library of Congress Control Number: 2019936212

Printed and bound in Malaysia, August 2020
ISBN: 978-1-61067-998-5